W9-ASU-965

Cristina Keeps a Promise

Virginia Kroll

illustrated by **Enrique O. Sanchez**

Albert Whitman & Company, Morton Grove, Illinois

For Colleen Quinn and Kaitlin MacNeil.—V.K.

To Aily Nash—E.O.S.

The Way I Act Books:

Cristina Keeps a Promise • Forgiving a Friend • Good Neighbor Nicholas

Honest Ashley • Jason Takes Responsibility • Ryan Respects

The Way I Feel Books:

When I Care about Others • When I Feel Angry

When I Feel Good about Myself • When I Feel Jealous

When I Feel Sad • When I Feel Scared • When I Miss You

Library of Congress Cataloging-in-Publication Data

Kroll, Virginia L.
Cristina keeps a promise / written by Virginia Kroll ; illustrated by Enrique O. Sanchez.
p. cm. – (Way I act books ; 6)
Summary: Having promised her younger brother that she will watch him race in the Special Olympics, Cristina is offered the chance
to meet a famous author–her favorite–on the same day and must make a tough choice.
ISBN-13: 978-0-8075-1350-7 (hardcover)
ISBN-10: 0-8075-1350-4 (hardcover)
[1. Promises–Fiction. 2. Special Olympics–Fiction. 3. Conduct of life–Fiction.] I. Sanchez, Enrique O., 1942- ill. II. Title. III. Series.
PZ7.K9227Cri 2006 [E]–dc22 2006000123

Printed in the United States of America.
10 9 8 7 6 5 4 3 2 1

The design is by Carol Gildar.

For more information about Albert Whitman & Company, please visit our web site at www.albertwhitman.com.

"Watch me, Cristina! Watch me, Abby!" Victor, Cristina's little brother, raced around the playground. He was practicing for the Special Olympics.

"I'm watching. You sure are fast!" Cristina said.

"You go, Victor!" Abby, Cristina's cousin, shouted.
She was staying overnight with Cristina.

Cristina's best friend, Lisa, rode up on her bike. Cristina noticed that Lisa seemed sad. "What's wrong?" she asked her while Abby was timing Victor.

Lisa's lower lip trembled. "My parents are getting divorced," she whispered. "I just had to tell someone. But Mom doesn't want everyone knowing yet, so don't tell anyone else, okay?"

"I won't. I promise." Cristina crossed her heart.

When they were getting ready for bed, Abby said, "Lisa was really quiet today. I wonder if something's wrong."

Cristina shrugged and kept brushing her teeth. She wanted to tell Abby about Lisa's parents and the divorce. But Lisa had said, "Don't tell anyone yet," and Cristina had promised. She was glad that Abby didn't mention it again.

Cristina went to Victor's room for his goodnight hug. Victor said, "You're gonna be there for my race, right, Cristina?"

"I'll be there—I promise," Cristina said. Victor clapped, and Cristina hugged him tightly. "Sleep well, buddy."

Three days later, Lisa raced to Cristina's house. She wore a
huge smile, and Cristina was glad to see her looking happy.
"Cristina, guess what! Edward Atherton is coming to the book-
store where my mother works! We can meet him! Mom's in
charge of his book-signing, and we're going to take him out to
lunch! And you can come!"

Cristina's heart pounded. She and Lisa had read every one
of Edward Atherton's "Unicorn Castle" mysteries. He was so
famous, and now he was going to be at the very store where
Lisa's mother worked! "I can't believe it!" Cristina said. "Tell your
mom thanks a million, trillion, zillion! Ooh, I can't *wait!*"

That night, Cristina went to the library and checked out some of Edward Atherton's books. She wanted to reread them before she met him.

Every day, between reading mysteries, Cristina helped
Victor practice for the race. "You're a winner," she told him.
Every time she said that, Victor laughed.

Two Fridays later, after school, Lisa asked, "Cristina, aren't you excited about tomorrow?"

"I sure am," Cristina answered. "And Victor is, too!"

Lisa frowned. "Victor? I didn't know he was going."

Cristina laughed. "Of course he's going," she said. Then she put two and two together. "Wait, Lisa. You mean . . . ?"

Lisa said, "Yeah, I mean the book-signing. It's tomorrow."

"So is the Special Olympics," Cristina said. "I promised Victor I'd go. I never even thought about the date."

"Oh, no," moaned Lisa. "What are you going to do?"

Cristina felt sick. "I don't know. I'll call you tonight."

That night at supper, Cristina felt as if she had swallowed squirmy worms instead of burritos.

When Victor had left the table, she blurted, "Mom, Dad— I know I told Victor I'd go to his race, but the Special Olympics is every year. I'll *never* get another chance to meet Edward Atherton! What should I do?"

"It's up to you, Cristina," Dad said.

Mom nodded. "You have to decide."

For a moment, Cristina's mind spun faster than a merry-go-round. *Victor or Atherton? Atherton or Victor?* Finally she made her decision and went to the phone.

"Great, Cristina!" Lisa said. "See you tomorrow."

The next morning, Cristina dressed in her pink unicorn shirt instead of her special gold "Victor" shirt.

Victor bounded out of his room. "Cristina, hurry, put your gold shirt on. I'm the fastest! I'm gonna win a medal, Cristina. You cheer real loud, okay? I'm gonna go practice." He dashed outside before Cristina could answer.

Cristina felt awful. Her decision didn't seem so simple now. It had been easy to keep her promise to Lisa. She still hadn't told anyone about the divorce. Why was *this* promise so much harder to keep?

Mom called out, "We're leaving in five minutes."

Cristina ran to the phone. When Lisa answered, Cristina said, "I'm really sorry—I just can't go with you. Victor's so excited, and I can't break my promise to him."

Lisa was disappointed, but she said, "Know what, Cristina? I'm glad you're keeping your promise."

Cristina whipped off her pink shirt and scrambled to put the gold one on. As she ran to the car, Victor shouted and clapped his hands. "Cheer real loud, promise?"

Cristina smiled as she buckled herself in. "Yes, buddy, I promise," she said, and she meant it with all her heart.

Cristina did cheer loudly. And Victor came in first!

Afterwards, he ran up to Cristina and said, "I did it, Cristina! I told you!"

"I'm so proud of you, Victor!" Cristina said, hugging him.

I'm so glad I was here, she thought to herself.

When Cristina got home, a surprise was waiting at the
front door. It was a copy of Edward Atherton's brand-new
book. Inside was a message:

To Cristina,
who keeps her
promises —
Hooray for you!
Best wishes,
Edward Atherton